D1112297

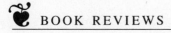 ## BOOK REVIEWS

Here's what people are saying:

. . . Frances Zweiffel's text moves along swiftly and the black pencil and color wash cartoons by Whitney Darrow, Jr. are appropriately lively . . .

from SCHOOL LIBRARY JOURNAL

. . . Kim finds what true love is in this book that is a sort of Born Free *for Squirrels. . .*

from the HOUSTON CHRONICLE

A good-natured account, based on the author's experiences. . . . Steers would-be pet raisers in the right direction.

from KIRKUS REVIEWS

For Dick,

who always understands about pets

This book is a presentation of Weekly Reader Books.
Weekly Reader Books offers book clubs for children from
preschool through high school.

For further information write to:
Weekly Reader Books
4343 Equity Drive
Columbus, Ohio 43228

Library of Congress Cataloging in Publication Data
Zweifel, Frances W.
    Bony.

    (An I can read book)
    SUMMARY: When his squirrel creates havoc as a house
pet, Kim teaches Bony to be an outside squirrel.
    [1. Squirrels—Fiction] I. Darrow, Whitney, date
II. Title.
PZ7.Z85Bo3   [E]   76-58688
ISBN 0-06-027070-5
ISBN 0-06-027071-3 lib. bdg.

Weekly Reader Books presents

BONY

by FRANCES ZWEIFEL

Pictures by WHITNEY DARROW, Jr.

An I CAN READ Book ®

HARPER & ROW, PUBLISHERS
New York, Hagerstown, San Francisco, London

It was summer.

Kim stood in his backyard

and listened to bees humming

in the flowers.

Then Kim heard a squeak.
Something dropped to the ground
near a big oak tree.

It was a baby squirrel!

Its eyes were shut tight.

It squeaked and squeaked.

Mom came to see

what Kim was holding.

"A baby squirrel!" she said.

"Where is its mother?"

There were no other squirrels

in the yard.

"I saw a dead squirrel

on the road," Kim said.

The baby squirrel squeaked again.

"Poor little one," Mom said.

"It must be very hungry."

"What can we feed it?" asked Kim.

"Milk," said Mom,

"mixed with some warm water."

They went into the kitchen.

Mom mixed the milk in a cup,

and found an eyedropper.

Kim held the baby squirrel

on his lap.

He took the eyedropper

and fed milk to the baby squirrel.

It drank all the milk.

Then it curled up in Kim's lap

and went to sleep.

Kim held the baby carefully.

How little it was!

"Mom," he said,

"may I keep this baby squirrel

for a pet?"

"Squirrels belong outside,"

his mother said.

"They are not good inside pets."

"Please, Mom!" said Kim.

"It will die outside all alone!"

"Yes," said Mom slowly.

"You are right.

You may keep the baby

squirrel for a while,

until it can take care of itself."

Kim smiled down at the

little squirrel.

"What shall I name it?" he wondered.

The baby squirrel was very thin.

It had almost no fur on its body.

"It looks like skin and bones.

I'll name my squirrel Bony,"

Kim told his mother.

"We must give Bony a warm nest,"

Mom said.

Kim found some rags.

He made a soft nest for Bony

in a shoe box.

"Is Bony a boy or a girl?"

he asked.

Mom picked up the squirrel.

"Bony is a female," she said.

"Bony has her eyes closed,"

said Kim.

"Is she blind?"

"No," said Mom.

"Many baby animals

cannot open their eyes

until they are several weeks old."

Bony slept, and squeaked for food,

and then slept some more.

Each time Kim fed her,

he gently rubbed her fur clean

with a cloth.

Bony grew very fast.

Now she was not so thin.

Soon her body was covered

with soft fur.

After ten days,

Bony opened her eyes.

She climbed all over Kim.

Wherever Kim went in the house,

Bony went too.

Bony still drank milk,

but now she ate other food,

like Cheerios and fruit and nuts.

One day Bony took Kim's candy bar.

She climbed up the curtains with it.

When Kim yelled at her,

Bony dropped some of the candy

on his head.

She hid nuts

behind the sofa cushions,

and raisins under the rug.

Bony ate peanuts in Kim's bed.

When Kim went to sleep at night,

his bed felt crunchy.

Kim asked Dad, "Why does Bony

hide her food?"

"Grown squirrels hide their food

to store it for winter," Dad said.

"Bony is growing up."

Bony liked to play hide-and-seek.

She hid in the pocket of Kim's robe.

She hid in dresser drawers.

Bony liked to play bite-the-foot

with Kim.

When Kim put one foot out of bed,

Bony would jump on the foot

and pretend to fight it.

Bony liked to help Mom

in the kitchen.

Mom made fancy cookies

with nuts on top.

When the cookies were cooling,

Bony took all the nuts.

Autumn came, with cool weather.

Acorns fell from the oak trees.

Kim brought some acorns to his pet.

Bony dug up Mom's houseplants

and buried the acorns in the pots.

Plants and dirt were scattered

all over the rug.

Mom scolded the squirrel.

Bony climbed up the curtains

and scolded back.

Kim laughed so hard

he had the hiccups.

But Mom did not laugh.

"Kim," she said,

"I like your pet.

But I like my houseplants too.

Bony must not dig up my plants!"

"But, Mom!" said Kim.

"All squirrels bury acorns."

"Not in our house," said Mom.

"Bony should live outside now."

"Oh, Mom!" cried Kim.

"Not yet!

Bony is still too little!"

"Pretty soon, then," said Mom.

When school began,

Bony had to stay home alone.

She played in Kim's room.

After a while, she went to sleep.

When Kim came home,

he found his room in a mess.

The pencils were all chewed up.

There were tooth marks

on the chair.

And Kim's best model boat

was chewed to pieces.

Kim saw Bony asleep on his bed.

"Bony!" Kim shouted.

"You bad squirrel!"

Mom came running.

"What's wrong?" she asked.

"My best boat!" he shouted.

"Bony chewed my best boat
to pieces!

She is a bad squirrel!"

"But, Kim," Mom said,

"Bony didn't know it was a model.

She gnawed it because
it was made of wood."

Kim was still angry.

"Look at my pencils! And my chair!

Why does Bony have to gnaw

things made of wood?" he asked.

"Squirrels must gnaw

on hard things," Mom said.

"Their teeth grow all the time.

Bony must gnaw

to wear down her teeth."

"But I liked that model boat,"

Kim said.

Bony was hiding under the covers.

She was shaking with fear.

Kim felt sorry for her.

"You aren't really a bad pet,"

he said.

"You were only being a squirrel."

Kim picked up Bony and cuddled her.

"Mom," he said. "I love Bony.

But she isn't really

a good inside pet."

Mom said, "Bony is grown up.

Maybe it is time for her to be

an outside squirrel."

"Yes," said Kim.

He took Bony to the big oak tree.

Bony climbed up the tree

a little way.

But when Kim walked back

to the house, Bony ran after him.

"Bony doesn't know how to be an outside squirrel," Kim said.

"She would be cold and hungry outside!"

Mom thought for a minute.

"We must teach her to live outside, like the wild squirrels."

"What can we do?" Kim asked.

"Dad can build a home for her,"
Mom said.

"And I can put food outside,"
Kim said.

That night, Dad made a nest box.

He cut a hole in front for a door.

Kim put soft rags

and nuts and raisins in the box.

The next morning,

Dad and Kim nailed the box

high up in the oak tree.

When Kim took Bony to the box,

she went inside

and looked out of the door.

Bony stayed in the oak tree

all that day.

But at night,

she came back to the house.

The door was shut.

Bony could not get inside.

So she gnawed on the door.

Kim let Bony come inside.

The next morning, Dad said,

"Bony must stay outside.

If she comes in the house again,

we will take her far away."

In the morning

Kim took Bony back to the oak tree.

He had never felt so bad.

His chest hurt,

and tears made his eyes sting.

"Please, Bony," he whispered,

"please be an outside squirrel!"

Then he had to go to school.

All day, Bony played

near the oak tree.

After school, Kim looked for her.

She was hunting for acorns

on the ground.

Suddenly Kim saw another squirrel.

It was the same size as Bony.

Bony saw the other squirrel too.

She sat up straight.

Her tail flipped up and down.

She ran up the oak tree

and scolded the new squirrel.

Then the new squirrel ran after her!

They stopped, and touched noses.

The two squirrels played in the tree.

Kim put some peanuts on the ground.

Bony came down and ate a peanut.

The new squirrel did not come down.

Kim went into the house

and watched from the window.

At last, the new squirrel

came down the tree too.

He took a peanut up to the nest box.

Then Bony took a peanut up.

After the two squirrels put

all the peanuts into the box,

they went inside the box too.

In bed that night,

Kim heard scratching sounds

at the window.

He stopped breathing to listen.

Was it Bony trying to come inside?

No, it was only the wind blowing

dry leaves against the window.

Finally Kim fell asleep.

The next morning, before breakfast,

Kim ran to the oak tree.

He saw the two squirrels sitting

on the nest box eating peanuts.

"Hi, up there!" Kim called.

Bony stopped eating.

She looked over the edge of the box

and dropped a peanut shell

on Kim's head.

Kim laughed as he ran back to
the house.

"Mom! Dad! Come look!" he shouted.

"Bony is an outside squirrel!"

AUTHOR'S NOTE

We raised two baby squirrels whose mother had
died. The babies were about three weeks old when
we found them. We fed them with an eyedropper.
This is the mixture they drank:

> 1 teaspoon evaporated milk
>
> 3 teaspoons warm water
>
> a tiny pinch of sugar

When the squirrels were four weeks old, we
mixed some baby cereal with the milk mixture.
Every day, we put a little more cereal in the milk.
The little squirrels grew strong and healthy
and frisky.